WEBSITE OF THE
WARPED WIZARD

# WEBSITE OF THE WARPED WIZARD

BY **ERIC A. KIMMEL**

ILLUSTRATED BY **JEFF SHELLY**

**DUTTON CHILDREN'S BOOKS** NEW YORK

Text copyright © 2001 by Eric A. Kimmel
Illustrations copyright © 2001 by Jeff Shelly

*Library of Congress Cataloging-in-Publication Data*
Kimmel, Eric A.
Website of the warped wizard / by Eric A. Kimmel;
illustrated by Jeff Shelly.—1st ed.     p.   cm.
Summary: Jess and her friend Matthew find themselves
drawn into a computer game in which they must defeat an evil wizard
in order to save a friendly centaur and an elf, as well as King Arthur
and some of his companions.
ISBN 0-525-46656-8
[1. Computer games—Fiction.   2. Characters in literature—Fiction.]
I. Shelly, Jeff, ill. II. Title. PZ7.K5648 We 2001 [Fic]—dc21 00-058688

Published in the United States by Dutton Children's Books,
a division of Penguin Putnam Books for Young Readers
345 Hudson Street, New York, New York 10014
www. penguinputnam.com

Designed by Alan Carr
Printed in USA • First Edition
1   3   5   7   9   10   8   6   4   2

*For Jess and Matt*
E.A.K.

# CONTENTS

WEBSITE OF THE
# WARPED WIZARD

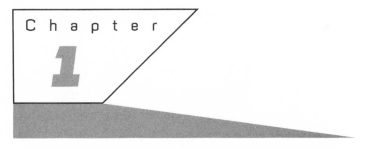

# The Game Begins

"Oh, crabcakes! Not again!" Jessica Lyons shrieked as her computer monitor turned red. "I hate those gophers. They're killing me."

They certainly were—four times in the last twenty minutes. Jessica was playing a video game on her computer. A game called Gopher. It was supposed to be simple, but it wasn't. The idea was to clear a field of mutant gophers by dropping blaster bombs down their holes.

The first levels were easy. The gophers didn't do anything except squeak when they got blown up or sliced into mincemeat under Jessica's riding lawn mower. But once Jessica reached the higher levels, the gophers began fighting back. They popped up behind her with machine guns, bazookas, and a laser cannon. They came at her with chain saws. They even tossed back her blaster bombs.

Jessica's only chance was to find the key to the gasoline pump, flood their tunnels with gasoline, and burn them out. But she couldn't find the key. Meanwhile, the gophers kept blasting, and Jessica kept hitting the **<Replay>** button to try again.

Suddenly, the phone rang. Jessica picked up the receiver. "Who is this?" she asked, none too pleasantly.

"Hi, Jess! What are you doing?" It was her friend Matthew.

"None of your business," Jessica snapped.

"Are you playing Gopher again?"

"How did you know?"

"You always get in a bad mood when you play Gopher."

"I'm not in a bad mood. I just don't like to have my concentration interrupted by annoying phone calls. I have to focus. This is a challenging game."

"Gopher? Are you kidding? It's a baby game. All you have to do is find the key to the gasoline pump. It's under—"

"STOP! I don't need any help. I can find it myself."

"Well, if you change your mind, type in the cheat code **<45-128-makemeimmortal>**, and you'll never die, no matter what the gophers throw at you."

"I never stoop to using cheat codes." Jessica sniffed. "Unlike some people I know. If I need hints, I'll go to the **<cheatgames>** website."

"There's nothing wrong with looking for help if you need it," said Matt. "Besides, if you never cheat, how do you know about that website?"

"Never mind."

"Here's why I called," Matthew said. "Forget Gopher. I just found this killer website that is way cool. Honest, Jess! It's the most amazing thing I have ever seen on the Internet. You've got to check it out. Write this down: **<www.go4.com//web adventures>**."

Jessica scribbled the web address on the back of her hand. "Well, maybe I'll check it out sometime."

"Not sometime. Now!" Matt insisted. "Quit Gopher and log on to that website. You won't be sorry. I'll meet you there in five minutes."

"Meet me where?"

*Click.* Matthew hung up.

What was that all about? Jess wondered. Something about the mysterious website made her uneasy. Jess knew there were scary places on the Internet where kids didn't belong. Maybe she should check it out, just to make sure Matt wasn't getting into anything weird. Besides, being blown up and machine-gunned by gophers was getting boring.

Jess pulled down the menu from the top of the screen and hit **<Quit>** to exit the game. She doubleclicked the Door icon on her computer desktop to connect to the Internet. The modem hummed, buzzed, whirred, beeped. It made noises like a cat, a frog, an old man clearing his throat. It did everything but log on.

"Come on! Don't take all day!" Jess muttered. She sounded like her mom, stuck in traffic on the freeway. Her home page appeared after a few minutes. "You have mail!" a friendly computer voice chirped.

"Can't bother with that now," said Jess.

She typed in **<www.go4.com//webadventures>** and hit **<Enter>**.

The monitor immediately turned blank. A LOAD-ING message came on the screen. Loading, loading, loading. Music began to play—a squeaky, annoying little tune. Then a cartoon gopher in a cowboy hat appeared, dancing in a herky-jerky computer-movie fashion.

"Hi, kiddos!" the gopher said in a voice that was just as squeaky and annoying as the music. "I'm Garth Gopher! Do you want to have fun, fun, fun? Well, you've come to the right place, kiddos. Fun, fun, fun is what Webadventures is all about." Then he began singing a song about fun and friends and love and rainbows and whales and unicorns and puppies and kittens and ponies and peace and happiness and making dreams come true.

"I wish I had some blaster bombs to throw at him." Jessica tapped her foot impatiently as the gopher finished the song and began his programmed speech. "Hurry up! Get to the point!"

The point, when he finally got to it, was that this website had been created by GO-4 Research & Development, a scientific foundation created to test new kinds of computer games. The computer experts at the foundation needed real kids to try out their games to see if they work. They also needed to learn what kids really like.

"So let's help out Ms. Scientist and her terrific team. After all, they're doing this all for you, kiddos!" Garth Gopher said. "Why? Because the friendly scientists and business executives at GO-4 love kids! We want all our little friends to be happy, happy, happy all the time."

"Like making big bucks has nothing to do with it," Jessica sneered.

Garth Gopher stopped in midsentence. "Did you say something, little girl?"

Jessica gulped. Was that silly gopher talking to her?

Garth smiled. "No? My mistake. Perhaps *you* would like to try our game?"

"Uh . . . sure!" Jessica stammered.

"Good! You'll be glad you did, because I know you're going to have fun, fun, fun! Playing our game is very simple. Just follow the directions. If you become confused, frightened, or wish to quit the game at any time, type: **<46589782436~~// grinkiskis/jaszarokszallas_8.11.5>.** Got that?"

"Got it," Jessica answered.

"Groovy! Begin whenever you're ready."

The screen dissolved, taking Garth with it. A deep voice echoed:

*"You are about to begin the greatest virtual adventure of all. Don your armor and your sword. Your Virtual Quest is about to begin!"*

An iron gate appeared with the word

## Enter

written across it in crusty yellow letters. *It looks like the entrance to a castle,* Jessica thought as she clicked on it.

The monitor and all the lights in her room went dark. Jessica sat very still. "Uh-oh! Did I do that?" The lights returned. Jessica was still at her desk—only it wasn't her desk. In place of the clutter of pens and pencils, she saw a dusty bottle of ink and a kind of feather that she guessed might be a quill pen. A suit of black armor stood where her clothes closet should have been. A battered shield hung on the opposite wall in place of the bulletin board filled with pictures of Chilli, T-Boz, and Left-Eye, the singers of Jess's favorite group, TLC.

"This could be my room, but it is definitely not my stuff. Okay, what's going on?" Jessica said out loud. Looking up, she noticed that the CD player on top of her bookcase had also vanished. In its place lay a stringed instrument that resembled a guitar, except it had lots more strings and a pear-shaped body.

"Who plays that? Not me!" Jessica glanced at the monitor. The castle door still filled the screen, except the word on it now was <**Welcome!**>

"Welcome to where?" Jessica asked herself. "Thanks, but I don't plan on sticking around. This

place is too creepy for me. I want my room back."
She searched the screen for an **<Exit>** button.
"Okay, where is it? How about **<Back>, <Return>,
<Escape>, <Quit>.** I'm not fussy. Whatever gets me
out of here."

Suddenly she froze. Looking at the monitor, she
saw the suit of armor across the room reflected onto
the screen. "I didn't see that. It didn't move. This
isn't happening."

Jessica whirled in her chair as the armored figure
came clanking toward her.

# Chapter 2

# The Armory

"EEEEEEEEEEEEEE!!!!!!"

The armored figure clanked to a halt. Its mailed gauntlet raised the visor on its helmet. A familiar face peeked out. "Don't be scared, Jess. It's me!"

"Matthew! What are you doing in that outfit?"

"It's armor, Jess. I put it on. It fits perfectly. Isn't it cool?" Matthew unsheathed his sword. "I am Sir Matthew the Lionhearted! Bring on the dragons! I will slay them."

Jessica rolled her eyes. "Would you mind getting out of that iron jumpsuit before you break something. You look like a walking can of cat food. Where are we, anyway? What is this place?"

Matthew began unbuckling pieces of armor. "We're in the Armory."

"Well, duh!" Jessica said. "Where else do you go for armor? But why do we need it?"

"For the quest!"

"What quest?"

"The quest we're going on. That's the point of the game."

"What do we have to do?"

"I don't know. The quest hasn't begun. You begin the quest by finding out what you're questing for. It's all in the *Read Me* file. Didn't you read it?"

"No," Jessica replied. "Nobody reads Read Me files."

"Then why are they there?"

"So that when the program doesn't work, you'll think you messed up because you didn't read the file and won't blame the development company for putting out a crummy piece of software."

"Don't worry, Jess. This is no crummy piece of

software," Matthew said. "I've been exploring the website. Everything's so real! You hardly know you're playing a game. It's like you stepped into the screen."

"So fill me in," said Jessica. "What happens first?"

"First, we prepare for our quest by coming to the Armory to choose the equipment we think we'll need."

"Okay, so where do we get our quest stuff?"

"It's all on-line!" Matthew clicked the castle door pictured on the monitor. It swung open, accompanied by the sound of squeaking hinges.

"Wow!" Jessica exclaimed.

A long hallway appeared. Swords, clubs, and battle-axes of every shape and size hung on the walls. "You use the mouse to navigate down the hall," Matt explained. "When you see something you like, you click on it. That's how I got my sword and armor."

"Got anything more modern?" Jessica asked. "I'm not into heavy metal."

Matthew pulled down a menu from the top of the screen and highlighted the word *Guide*. A map showing a maze of corridors appeared on the screen. Matthew clicked in the upper-right corner. The screen instantly changed. The hall looked the same, but the weapons were definitely not medieval.

"That's more like it!" Jessica moved the mouse around in all directions, clicking on everything in sight. Whenever <Add to your shopping basket?> appeared on the screen, she clicked <Yes>.

"Jess? What are you doing?" Matthew asked.

"Firepower, Matt! It's how wars are won."

"Mortars? Blaster bombs? Rocket launchers? Stinger missiles? What are we going to do with all this junk?"

"We going to blast anyone who gets in our way. It will be a short quest."

"But, Jess—!"

"Okay, okay! I'll cancel the Phantom jets and the aircraft carrier. Satisfied? Now, let's see . . . I click here to send the order."

"Jess! Look out!" Matthew pulled Jessica aside as

a panel in the ceiling opened. A huge crate dropped down from overhead. It landed with a crash that shook the castle walls.

"What was that?"

"I think it's your order."

Matthew and Jessica pried open the enormous box. Inside, they found a huge assortment of weapons.

"Wow!" Jessica exclaimed. "This *is* a lot of stuff. I'm glad I canceled the aircraft carrier."

"How are we going to carry it all?" Matthew asked.

"Good question," said Jessica. "Back to the catalog." She checked the pull-down menu again. "Let's see . . . *Nuclear Weapons* . . . *Chemical and Biological Warfare* . . . Here it is! *Transport!*"

Pictures of vehicles of all shapes and sizes filled the screen. "We'll just order ourselves a Humvee. I told you it's simple."

"We don't know how to drive," Matt said.

"Cancel the Humvee. Helicopter?"

"We don't know how to fly."

"What about this one over here?" Jessica clicked on a folder labeled *Myths and Legends*.

A different set of pictures appeared. "That's it! Just what we need! The perfect solution!" Jessica whizzed the pointer arrow down a row of illustrations and clicked.

"Medusa? We don't want Medusa!" Matt covered his eyes. "What did you do that for, Jess! We're going to turn to stone!"

"Uncover your eyes, silly! I didn't order anybody who's going to turn us to stone. Or any one-eyed giants, either."

"What did you select?"

"You'll see." Jessica glanced at her watch. "I expect delivery any minute now."

A tremendous *thud!* hit the door. Matthew jumped. "What was that?"

"Special delivery!" Jessica jumped up from the computer. She opened the door.

"Cool!" Matt exclaimed. "It's a centaur!"

A half-man/half-horse creature stood in the doorway. It definitely didn't look like the ones pictured in mythology books. This centaur wore a purple tank top on his human front and, on his horse behind, a pair of baggy shorts that came all the way down to his hocks. A leather thong gathered his hair into a long, blond ponytail that matched his other tail in back. He wore a backward-facing cap with a *Surf's Up!* logo. A pair of designer sunglasses shaded his eyes. He carried a square vinyl package with the words ROMEO'S PIZZA printed on top.

"Are you the dudes who ordered the double pepperoni and pineapple?" the centaur asked.

"I don't know about pizza. We ordered you," Jessica stammered.

"Pizza comes with it. Today's special is Hawaiian Holiday. Trust me, dudes. It's good! Where do you want it?"

"On that table. Next to the armor," Jessica said.

"Whatever you say, babe," the centaur drawled as he trotted by.

"Why do you wear pants?" Matthew asked.

"Same reason you do, little buddy. Nobody needs to know my business. Or see it. Say, dudes! It's almost lunchtime, and I still haven't had my break. How about if I chow down with you?"

"Sure!" Matt said.

It was a large pie, so there was plenty of pizza for Matt and Jess, even through the centaur ate half of it.

"He eats like a horse!" Matt whispered to Jessica.

"Be glad he's only half a horse. Otherwise, he'd eat the rest," Jess whispered back.

"I heard that, amigos. Hey, can I help it if I get hungry? The way I'm built, I can't exactly pig out on hay." The centaur let out a thundering burp.

"Gross!" Jessica said.

"Can't help it, honeybunch. It's my animal nature. Be glad it wasn't the other end."

Matthew began to giggle. "He's cool!"

The centaur laughed. "My man! Give me five!" He and Matthew slapped hands. "What's your name, little bud?"

"Matt. And this is my friend Jessica."

"Super to meet you, dudes. I'm Dennis."

"That's a dumb name for a guy who's half-horse!" Jessica snapped.

"Beats Trigger!" Dennis polished off the pizza crusts. "So, saddle pals, let's get down to business. You ordered a centaur from mythsRus.com. Any special reason? You want to admire my physique? You want to do some barrel racing? You want to 'horse' around? Nyuk, nyuk!"

"We need you to help on our quest," Jessica explained.

"Awesome! Where are we going? Maui? Acapulco?"

"We don't know yet. You have to carry our stuff."

"What stuff?"

"That stuff." Jessica pointed to the weapons pile.

Dennis gasped. "Whoa! You'd need an elephant to lug all that junk! What do you think I am, a mule?"

"Okay, cool your jets. I'll order a wagon if it's such a big deal."

"No way, hon!" Dennis pulled a booklet out of his pocket. He handed it to Jessica. "Here's the contract, duly negotiated and agreed to by the Centaurs Union, Local 384. I call your attention to page twenty-eight, paragraph five. Read it!" Dennis recited the lines by heart. "Centaurs are not required to pull or carry burdens in excess of two hundred pounds."

"You weigh eighty, Jess. I'm sixty-five." Matt calculated the sum on his fingers. "That only leaves fifty-five pounds for equipment. Unless we want to walk."

Jessica started pulling weapons from the pile. "We're not walking. Take out the grenades . . . rocket launcher . . . ground-to-air missile . . . submachine gun . . . How am I doing?"

"Still two pounds over. But who's counting?"

"What about me?" Matt wailed. "Don't I get to take anything?"

"Sure you do, little dude." Dennis reached into his backpack. He pulled out a glowing stick and tossed it into midair. It floated to Matt's hand.

Matt held it tight, as if it might fly away. "It's a magic wand!"

"Good guess, O wise one," Dennis said. "I got it on my last job. I rode around with Harry, this English kid. I forget his last name: Trotter, Rotter.

Something like that. Sweet little guy, but really into his wizard thing. Bit of a noo-noo, if you know what I mean." Dennis whirled his finger in front of his ear.

"A real magic wand! What does it do?"

"Whatever you want."

Jessica sniffed. "Okay, I'm taking the rocket launcher, the Uzi, and the blaster bombs."

"Not so fast. Let me call your attention to page nine, paragraph seventeen. 'Centaurs are not required to carry weapons inconsistent with the era of the specific quest.' In other words, guys, if they didn't have it back then, you don't get to have it now."

"Great!" Jess snapped. "There goes everything. We're defenseless."

"What about that crossbow?" Matt pointed to an ancient crossbow and quiver of crossbow bolts hanging from a hook on the wall.

"Excellent choice," said Dennis. "Fine workmanship. Low mileage. Long-term warranty."

"Don't rub it in," said Jess, slinging the quiver and crossbow over her shoulder.

"All set? Cowabunga! It's time to mount up, *compañeros*." Dennis stood still as Jessica helped Matt slide onto his back. She pulled herself up behind him.

"Tally-ho!" she yelled as they trotted through the doorway. Jess held on to Matt while Matt held tight to Dennis's ponytail.

"Quest-time, folks! Our adventure begins!"

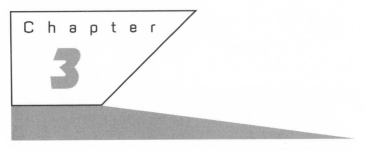

# Hard Times

Dennis trotted over the castle drawbridge and down a winding path that led them deeper and deeper into a dark, forbidding forest.

"This place gives me the creeps," Matt said, clutching his magic wand. "I hope my wand works if we need it."

"This'll work if that doesn't," said Jessica, patting the crossbow slung across her shoulder. "I remember learning on the History Channel that a crossbow could shoot an arrow through an inch of iron plate."

"What about a paper plate? Nyuk! Nyuk!" Dennis chuckled.

Jess sighed. "I'm talking about the History Channel, and he gives me Comedy Central. Brother! This is going to be a long quest. By the way, I assume you know where we're going. Didn't we pass that same tree an hour ago?"

"I hope we're not lost," said Matt.

"Relax, buds," Dennis replied as he clip-clopped along. He picked his way between the trees. "Where's your sense of adventure? There's nothing like getting lost in a forest to start a quest right."

Matt panicked. "Then we really are lost!"

"Chill, everybody. Trust me. I've made this quest a hundred times. And I never lost anyone. Well, that's not completely true. There was Justin, that redheaded kid. He just wouldn't listen. I told him to leave the unicorn alone."

"Unicorns are supposed to be friendly," Jessica remarked.

"Take it from me—they're not!"

"Well, how many questers have you lost?" Matt asked.

Dennis counted the casualties on his fingers. "Maybe fifteen. That's not too bad."

"It is if you're one of the fifteen," Jessica replied.

"That's nothing," Dennis continued. "You're lucky you didn't click on my girlfriend, Peg. She's one of those winged horses, you know? She loses questers right and left. She's always banging into power lines, broadcast towers. I think she needs glasses."

"I may need glasses, too," said Matt. "I think I see an elf."

It was indeed an elf, standing beneath one of the oak trees lining the path. This poor elf had definitely seen better days. Several days' growth of green stubble covered his chin. His emerald shorts hung loose, torn at the knees. His jacket's seams had split, and his hat was a shapeless clump of moss-colored felt with a bedraggled feather. The parchment sign that hung around his neck read:

*HOMELESS ELF*

*CRUSADE VETERAN*

*NO MONEY! NO JOB!*

*WILL WORK FOR FOOD*

"What do elves eat?" Matt asked Dennis.

"That one will eat anything he can get. Looks like he hasn't had a decent meal in a long time." The centaur stopped beside the tree. "What's happening, little green person? You look down on your luck. Or maybe your luck is down on you?"

The elf held out his hand. "Can you help me out, buddy? I'm hurting!"

"Sure thing, man!" Dennis took a handful of change from his pocket and pressed it into the elf's palm. He turned to Matt and Jessica. "How about a contribution? Strictly voluntary, but it's for a very worthy cause."

"Here's fifty cents," Matt said as he handed down two quarters. "I'm sorry I don't have more. Maybe this magic wand can help!" Matt waved it in the air. A banana appeared. It floated down into the elf's hand.

"Thanks, buddy! I like bananas." The elf turned to Jessica. "How about you, sweetheart? Got any spare change?"

"Not for you, you bum!" Jessica snapped. "And I'm not your sweetheart! Why don't you get a job?"

HOMELESS ELF
Crusade Veteran
No MONEY
No Job
WILL WORK for food

The elf's face turned dark green with anger. He pointed the banana at Jessica like an accusing finger. "You have some nerve, sister! Who do you think you are, sitting up there on your high horse—half-horse, anyway—looking down your nose at me? I'll have you know I used up a whole sack of goose quills and three jars of blackberry ink filling out job applications. Do you think I was always like this? I had a career once. I had respect, responsibility. Elves looked up to me. I used to be chief of security at Elf Acres, the biggest amusement park in Fairyland. The happiness and safety of thousands of visitors depended on me. Trolls and goblins would muscle their way into the park starting fights, knocking over the concession stands. When they needed someone to toss those losers out, who do you think they sent for? Me! It was a tough job, but an important one. And I loved it."

"Why did you quit?" Matt asked.

"I didn't quit," the elf replied. "I was fired. Canned. Laid off. Pink-slipped. A big corporation—GO-4 Enterprises—bought Elf Acres. Claimed they were going to make it bigger and better. Instead, they closed down the park and fired everyone who worked there. Then they bulldozed the place to make way for a mall."

"Malls are cool," said Jessica.

"You wouldn't think so if you were the one who got tossed out like . . . a banana peel! I worked there two hundred years. The best years of my life!"

"Elves live a long time," Dennis explained. "It was a bad scene, dudes. Not only elves got fired. Fairies, leprechauns, pixies, dwarfs, gnomes—they all lost their jobs. Elf Acres was an equal-opportunity employer. It was a big blow to the little green community."

"Why didn't they get new jobs at the mall?" Matt asked.

"Because the mall wouldn't hire us!" the elf snapped. "They said we were too short. And green didn't go with their corporate colors. I couldn't even get work as a burger flipper. You had to be tall enough to see over the counter."

"That's discrimination!" Jessica exclaimed.

"Tell me about it! We marched; we picketed; we filed complaints. No answer. I can't tell you how many days I spent cooling my buns at King Arthur's palace. It used to be anyone in Camelot could drop by and talk to the king. No more. Show up without an appointment, and the palace goons throw you out on your patootie. I'm beginning to wonder if King Arthur even cares. Maybe there is no King Arthur. Maybe he's like one of those dummies we had at the park. They dust him off for the parade, and when it's over, they shove him back in the garage."

"I don't know, little green guy. I'm sure King Arthur is real. And I'm sure he cares, way deep down in his heart of hearts," said Dennis. "The man may not be getting your message."

"He better start getting it! Things around here need to change. And fast, or there's gonna be a problem. If you run into the king, tell him I said so. Elfric the Elf. He'll remember me. Thanks for the banana, pal." The elf winked at Matthew as he began pulling off the peel. "It's nice to know some people still care."

"Don't mention it," Matt said.

Jessica's face turned red. "Okay, I apologize for

calling you a bum. I opened my mouth without thinking."

"You probably do that a lot, sister. I know you can't help it. But I don't take it personally. Everything's cool."

"Can I give you a blaster bomb to show I'm sorry?"

"What are you doing with a blaster bomb? We're in the Middle Ages. We're not even supposed to have gunpowder yet."

"I had it in my pocket," Jess explained. "I must have forgotten to take it out when we were back at the Armory."

"Hand it over," the elf said. "I'll turn it in for you. Want me to take that crossbow, too?"

"No way!"

Dennis shrugged. "I tried to tell her she doesn't need all the firepower. She won't listen. She thinks she needs to be armed to the teeth."

The elf nodded. "She'll learn."

"Learn what?" Jessica asked Dennis.

"You'll find out," the centaur said as they trotted along.

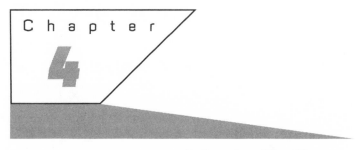

# Matt's Challenge

The narrow, twisting path led them deeper and deeper into the forest.

"Gosh!" Matthew exclaimed. "Look at these trees. They must be a thousand years old!"

"Double it and you'll be closer," Dennis said. "Some of our tree buddies have over eight thousand rings under their bark."

"Wow!" said Matt. "That's older than California redwoods!"

"That's a lot of patio furniture!" Jessica agreed. "Does anybody live here? Besides homeless elves, I mean?"

"Nobody you'd want to run into," Dennis replied.

"What's that?" Matt suddenly asked. Just up the path, hanging from the limb of a tree, he noticed an iron shield and an enormous horn. Underneath, someone had nailed a sheet of parchment to the tree's trunk.

"The ink's faded. It's hard to read. Can you make out what it says?" Matthew asked Jessica.

"I'll try." Jess slid down from the centaur's back. She stepped up to the tree for a better look. "It's written in funny old letters. Let's see . . . I think that's an *A*."

While Jessica studied the parchment, Matthew took down the shield and the horn. "These are old, too. I'll bet they're valuable. Who would leave antiques like this hanging from a tree in the middle of a forest?" Matt asked Dennis.

"Everything here is antique, Kemo Sabe," the centaur answered. "I've seen stranger things hanging from trees in the forest. You don't want to know about that. It would spoil your lunch."

"I think that I can read what it says," Jessica announced.

"Go on," said Matthew.

Jess began: "All Knights Who Cometh This Way, Taketh Thou ye Shield from ye Tree."

"Okay," said Matt. "I've got the shield."

"Bloweth Thou Three Times upon ye Horn."

"Like this?" Matt slung the shield over his shoulder. Raising the horn to his lips, he blew three times: TA-ROOO! TA-ROOO! TA-ROOOOOOOO!

"How was that?" he asked Dennis.

"Wynton Marsalis couldn't do better."

Jess continued. "Ye Black Knight Will Soon Appear to Do Battle unto Death."

"Huh?" said Matt. "What does that mean?"

"It means what it says, I guess," Jess answered. "Some character in black armor is going to show up and try to kill you."

"Why didn't you tell me that before I blew the horn?"

"Why didn't you wait until I finished reading?"

"Uh-oh! No time for squabbling, dudes. Company's here."

A terrifying knight in gleaming black armor came galloping up the path. He rode an enormous black charger and carried the biggest, ugliest club Matt had ever seen. It was as long as a baseball bat, with an iron ball studded with spikes fixed to its end. The knight reined in his charger.

"What ho, varlets! Prepare to do battle!"

"Jess! What do I do?" Matt squawked.

"I guess you have to fight him."

"How?"

"Any way you can."

"Aren't you going to help me?"

"I didn't blow the horn."

"Some friend you are!"

Dennis coughed. "You'd better pay attention, saddle pal. It's time to get your act together before we both get creamed. Hold on tight. Keep that shield between you and that club. And keep your fingers crossed. With luck, we'll both get out of this with our brains in one piece. Here he comes!"

"Here's where I get off," said Jess, ducking behind the tree.

The Black Knight charged at Matt. He rose in the stirrups and struck a mighty blow at Matt as he went galloping by. The iron shield rang like a bell. Matt's arm throbbed as if he'd been knocked on the funny bone. "Dennis! What do I do?" he screamed.

"Don't panic, little buddy! The dude's toast. Did you notice how he moves? Fat and slow. Hang on! We can take him."

"Are you kidding? Let's get out of here while we can!"

"No way, pal! Centaurs never run from a fight. Get ready. Here he comes. Use your magic wand!"

"How?"

"Stick it to him!"

The Black Knight galloped toward Matt again. As the thundering hoofbeats drew closer, Matt raised his shield and gripped his magic wand. At the last moment Dennis did a four-legged side step. The iron club descended—and missed. Matt leaned forward and tapped the magic wand against the knight's shoulder.

"Zounds!" he heard the Black Knight yell. "What sorcery is this? My arm! 'Tis frozen fast!" Try as he might, he could not raise his club. It was as if the armored joints in his right arm had suddenly become welded together. However, the magic worked only on that arm. The knight shifted the club to his left hand, wheeled his horse, and came at Matt again.

"Keep it up! He's scared now. I can tell!" Dennis shouted.

"Not as scared as I am!" Matt squeaked.

"Matt! I'm up here!" It was Jessica. She had climbed high into the tree's branches. Matt saw her aiming her crossbow. "I'm gonna wait till he gets closer so I don't miss," she said.

"If you wait any longer, it won't matter if you miss!" Matt yelled as the knight's iron club crashed against his shield.

*Whirrrr!* A crossbow bolt zipped past Dennis's ear. It struck the knight's helmet—*bong!*—and then ricocheted up into the tree.

"What, ho!" cried the knight. "My armor is enchanted by Merlin the Magician! I laugh at arrows, spears, and crossbows!"

"The dude won't be laughing long. Heads up!" said Dennis as a gray sphere the size of a basketball dropped out of the branches. Hornets! Jessica's bolt had cut loose their nest on the rebound. The nest scored a direct hit on the knight's helmet.

"AAAIIIIIEEEEEYYYYYYY!!!!!!" he screamed as the hornets swarmed into his armor. He flung himself from his horse and rolled back and forth on the ground.

"Cool! I think I won," Matt exclaimed.

"Yes!" crowed Jessica, thrusting her fist and waving her crossbow. "I did it with one shot!"

"Hey, dudes! Hate to spoil your fun, but the cat's in trouble. We need to do something," Dennis suggested.

"No way, man!" Jessica replied. "He tried to bash in Matt's head with a club. Serves him right."

"It's Matt's call," said Dennis. "What do you say, little buddy? He's a bad guy, I know. But we still ought to do the right thing."

"What should I do?" Matt asked.

"Try the magic wand. It hasn't let us down yet."

Matt slipped from Dennis's back. He pointed his

wand at the cloud of hornets swarming over the knight, then whirled it in a figure eight. The hornets followed the motion and flew in a figure eight of their own. Matthew pointed his wand straight up into the sky. The hornets launched themselves in the same direction, flying higher and higher in a funneling swarm until they disappeared.

"I yield, good sirs!" the Black Knight groaned. "I am fairly vanquished. I declare it. What doth thou require of me?"

"What does that mean?" Matthew asked Dennis.

"The dude caved. He's had enough. You beat him fair and square. Now he has to do anything you tell him to do. That's the rule of the school. The rite of the knight. The law of the claw. Get it?"

"I think so," said Matt. "What should I have him do?"

"I know! Make him eat worms!" said Jessica, climbing down from the tree. "Tell him he has to walk around the block in his underwear."

"That's cold!" said Dennis.

"Yeah!" Matt agreed. "And it won't get us anywhere. I have a better idea. Okay, Mr. Black Knight, take off your helmet. I want to see what you look like."

The knight rose to his feet slowly and removed the helmet from his head.

"Sweet!" Jess exclaimed. "He looks like the medieval version of Viola Swamp. Same hairdo."

"Satisfied?" the knight asked.

"Not yet," Matt replied. "Who set you up to this? Why are you challenging travelers coming through the forest? Tell the truth. We beat you fair and square."

"That's right, Knight," said Dennis. "You know the rule, fool!"

The Black Knight scowled. "Forsooth, it was Merlin the Magician. It was he who sendeth me here, with orders to let no one pass. He commanded me to peeleth my eyes for a boy and a girl riding a half-man, half-horse. I was to take them prisoner and escort them to Camelot."

"Can't say it's a case of mistaken identity. That description fits me and my buds to a T," Dennis said.

"But why?" Matthew asked. "What does Merlin want with us?"

The knight began to reply. "Merlin hath told me—"

"Hoo! Hoo! Hoo!" An owl perched high in the tree suddenly began hooting. More astonishing, it suddenly began talking. "Thou hath said quite enough, Sir Knight! Forsooth, thou flappeth thy jaw too much." The owl spread his wings. The Black Knight vanished. His empty armor remained standing for a moment, then collapsed. A tiny mouse ran out from the heap of metal. The owl swooped down and carried it off.

"Whoa! Did you see that? Was that creepy or what?" Jessica exclaimed.

"Thou hath had thy first encounter with the wizard Merlin." The Black Knight's horse, which had been peacefully grazing beside the path, lifted his head and spoke.

"This is very weird," said Matt.

"Are we related?" Dennis asked. "You remind me of my cousin Bob. From the back, anyway."

"I fear not," the horse replied in a sorrowful voice. "I am no true steed, or even half a steed, but an unfortunate soul bewitched into a horse's form by evil magic."

"Fear not, fellow equine. We'll find some way to break the spell. You're with friends now," said Dennis.

"If you're not really a horse, who are you?" Jessica asked.

The horse replied, "I, alas, was once a knight. The bravest of all the knights in King Arthur's court. They called me . . . Sir Lancelot!"

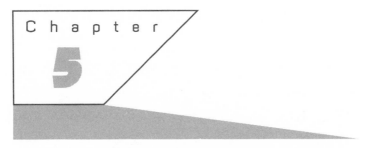

# The Not-So-Merrie Men

Jessica gasped. "I can't believe this! You're *the* Sir Lancelot? The greatest knight who ever lived? The hero of all the King Arthur stories? You're telling us that you're . . . a horse?"

"It must be true, Jess," said Matt. "We got it straight from the horse's mouth."

"Bummer!" Dennis exclaimed.

"Alas, Sir Centaur, thou knowest not what a true bummer is until thou hast been helpless in the hands of Merlin the Magician. I speaketh too much. Hark! I heareth noise in the distance. Someone approacheth! Rather, several someones approacheth."

Jessica listened. "I hear it, too. What is that noise? It sounds familiar."

"You're right!" said Matt. "If I didn't know we were in the Middle Ages, I'd say those were—"

"Bikers!" Dennis cried. A rough-looking crew on low-riding Harley-Davidsons came roaring through the trees. They wore green leather jackets emblazoned with a winged skull above two crossed arrows and the words: *Merrie Men M.C.—Sherwood Forest.*

"It's Robin Hood! We're saved! Robin Hood and his Merrie Men will help us. They rob from the rich and give to the poor. And right now, we're poor. Real poor! Hi, Robin! Hi, Maid Marian!" Matt called to the tough-looking biker riding in the lead and the equally tough-looking biker chick straddling the back of his Harley.

"Hey, kid! Great to see you!" Robin yelled back. His bike spun out clods of dirt as he ground to a halt. "Now, you and your pals—horses, too—throw your wallets, watches, gold chains, rings, credit cards, cell phones, laptop computers, and any other valuables that you have on the ground, and raise your hands in the air. Keep 'em high."

"Why?" Jessica asked.

" 'Cause this is a stickup."

"What? I can't believe this! We are being robbed by Robin Hood?"

"Why do you think they call him Robin?" The Merrie Men laughed.

"You're supposed to rob from the rich and give to the poor!" Matt protested. "That's what the books say."

"That's how it used to be," Robin replied. "Until we got smart. Now we're equal-opportunity outlaws. We rob from rich and poor alike. And we keep it! How do you think we paid for these Harleys?"

"This stinks!" said Jess. "You hold us up for what little we have so that you can ride those cool motorcycles while we have to creep along on smelly old horses?"

"I'll ignore that last remark," Dennis whispered.

"What's the matter, girlie?" sneered Little John,

the biggest, dumbest, and meanest-looking outlaw in Robin's band. "Are you jealous 'cause we have credit cards and you don't?"

"Who'd give credit cards to a bunch of thugs?" Jess shot back.

"Methinks I see-eth the hand of Merlin in this," Lancelot murmured.

"Of course you do!" Robin snapped. "Merlin's the guy with the brains. He's the one who got us credit cards and taught us how to use them. Know how we got these bikes? We ordered them over the Internet. Merlin did it for us. He's a genius, the man who set us straight! He's the one who told us to stop wasting our time giving handouts to bums and to get with the program. It's Merlin who's bringing Camelot into the New Age! In a few months, we'll all be part of the global economy. And about time, too! Big changes are coming. As Merlin says, 'You're either cruising the information superhighway or else you're roadkill.' "

"I don't like this scene one bit," said Dennis.

"I neither," Lancelot agreed.

"Who cares what two horses think? Enough chatter. Let's check out the swag." Robin glanced at the pitiful pile of loot that Matt, Jess, Dennis, and Lancelot had surrendered. It was hardly worth the effort of tallying: Lancelot's saddle and bridle, Dennis's backpack, Jessica's crossbow, a five-dollar bill, fifty-two cents in change, three Pokémon cards, and one magic wand.

"Why did you give up your magic wand?" Jessica hissed to Matt.

"What was I supposed to do?" Matt whispered back. "They told us to throw down everything!"

"Maybe they won't know what it is."

"Hey! Look at this, guys!" Little John picked up Matt's magic wand. He began waving it in the air.

"Look at me, Everybody! Hocus-pocus! I'm Merlin the Magician!"

"Quit horsing around, Little John!" Robin snapped. "Hand over that wand—*now!*"

"Oh yeah? Don't tell me what to do. I'm tired of you bossing us around all the time, Robin. I know how to shut you up. I'll turn you into a frog!" Little John pointed the wand at Robin.

"I said, give it to . . . Ribbit! Ribbit!"

Little John had turned him into a bullfrog.

"Now you've done it!" Maid Marian shrieked. She leaped off Robin's Harley and laid Little John out with one punch to the jaw.

"Don't you hit my Johnny!" yelled Maid Zelda, Little John's girlfriend. She head-butted Maid Marian into a tree.

"Ribbit! Ribbit!" croaked Robin. He hopped around underfoot, trying to avoid being squished by brawling Merrie Men and their ferocious Merrie Maidens, who began punching, bashing, kicking, stomping, and choking one another.

"Whoa! Mega-brawl!" cried Dennis. "This is better than wrestling!" He turned to Matt and Jess. "Okay, fellow captives. I recommend a quick change of scenery. Hop on one of those Harleys and make for splitsville. Lance and I will keep these turkeys busy."

"What about you?" Jessica asked. "We're not leaving our horse pals in danger!"

"Vexeth thee not thyself, fair maiden. The centaur and I will come to no lasting harm," Lancelot assured her.

"That's right, compassionate ones," Dennis agreed. "We're mythological. They can make us uncomfortable, but they can't do any permanent damage."

"But we don't know how to ride motorcycles!" Matt protested.

"Sure we do!" said Jess. "We wore the CD out playing Tomb Raider. If we could ride bikes with Lara Croft, we can ride them now."

"That was a video game!"

"This isn't? What's your problem, man?" asked Dennis.

"I give up," said Matt. "Let's go!"

Jess and Matt jumped aboard the biggest Harley they could see. Matt held tight while Jess kick-started the engine. The motor roared like a dinosaur coming to life.

"Hey! The brats are getting away!" the Merrie Men yelled. "After them!"

"Not so fast! It's party time, green outlaw dudes!" Dennis shouted as he and Lancelot charged into the melee. Matt and Jess caught a glimpse of Merrie Men and Merrie Maidens flying into the air as their two equine friends bucked and kicked. Jessica gave the Harley full throttle, and off they went, tearing down the forest path at top speed.

"This is awesome!" Jessica shrieked as they took turns in a shower of dirt and pebbles.

"I guess," Matt replied, keeping his eyes clamped shut. He didn't open them for a long while, until the Harley suddenly spun to a screeching stop. "What's going on?"

"Listen! Can you hear it?"

Matt cupped his hand to his ear. He heard the growling noise of motors in the distance.

"The Merrie Men must have gotten away from Lance and Dennis. I knew they couldn't hold them for long. What'll we do?" Jess asked.

"I have an idea," said Matt. "See those two signs up ahead where the path forks? One says: TO CAMELOT. The other says: DANGER! QUICKSAND! What do you say to switching them?"

"Way cool!" Jess agreed.

Making the switch took only a few seconds. Matt and Jess hid their bike behind the trees and waited

for the Merrie Men to roar by. Sure enough, they took the road into the swamp.

"We won't see them for a while. Maybe never, if we're lucky," said Jess.

"I hope Dennis and Lance are okay. Maybe we ought to go back to check. They might need our help," said Matt.

"No way! The only way we can help them or anybody else is to locate King Arthur and get to the bottom of whatever is going on in his kingdom. Let's hit it!"

Jess and Matt jumped back on the Harley. Soon they were roaring down the path to Camelot. They left the forest and began climbing higher and higher into the mountains.

"Jess, I think you should slow down," said Matt.

"What for? I'm having fun."

"Well, for one thing, this road is awfully narrow. There's a steep drop-off over the edge."

"Anything else?" Jess gunned the motor, sending the tachometer into the red zone as she down-shifted.

"It's full of potholes. We could hit a big bump and spin out."

"So?"

"Did you notice the sign we passed a mile back?"

"Yeah."

"Did you read what it said?"

"No."

"I did." Matt gulped. "It said: WARNING—BRIDGE OUT."

"EEEEEEEEEEEEEEEEEEEEEEEEEEEEEEEEEEE-EEEEEEEEEEEEE!!!!!!!!!!!!!" Jess screamed as the bike crashed through the barrier.

It was a long way down.

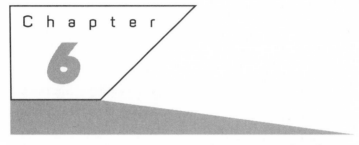

# The Good Place

Jessica opened her eyes. "Oh no! Here we go again! Where am I now?"

This was nothing like anywhere she'd ever been before. She could see no trees or buildings, only thick clouds of fleecy white vapor that took on different shapes as they passed. A chair went by, followed by a dragon, a dog, an old lady on a bicycle. For a moment Jess thought she recognized Dennis. She almost called to him before realizing that it was only a cloud in the shape of a centaur.

"Where am I?" Jessica was alone, as far as she

could tell. That thought made her uneasy. "Matt? Matthew! Where are you?" Jess called out.

Matt's head suddenly popped up from behind the billowing sail of a cloud boat. "I'm right here. Couldn't you see me?"

"How? It's like trying to look through cotton. Where are we, anyway? Do you have any idea what this place is?"

"Well, I have an idea," Matt said, "but I hope I'm wrong."

"What do you mean?"

"Well," Matt began, "considering we were going about a hundred twenty miles an hour when the bike flew off the bridge, I'd say we're dead."

"Really? Cool!"

"You're glad we're dead?"

"Sure! It's no big deal. We've gotten killed hundred of times playing computer games. Being dead just means you have to go back to Level One and start again. This is totally different. We're still in the game. We just have to figure out where in the game we are."

"I think I know," said Matt. "I don't smell anything burning—including us—so I'll bet we're in the good place. The one where nice people go."

"All right! How did we end up here?"

"In your case, I don't know. It could be a computer error."

"Let's hope they don't straighten it out any time soon. What's that floating above your head?"

Matt reached up. He pulled the golden ring down for a closer look. "I think it's a halo. You have one, too."

"Wow! Someone really did make a computer error! We better find out what's going on."

"Right! So we can find King Arthur," Matt said.

Jessica and Matt began walking along through the clouds. After a while they came to a tall gate made out of shiny iridescent material resembling pearls. An old man with a long white beard sat at a table, writing on a long scroll. He looked up as Jess and Matt approached.

"Names, please. I can't let you in unless your name is on our list."

"I'm Matthew. This is my friend Jessica. I'm not

sure how we got here. We were riding this motor-cycle—"

"Ah, yes! Here we are!" The man pointed to an entry at the end of the scroll. "Didn't read the sign. Didn't slow down. Went right through the barrier. That will get you here, all right."

"It wasn't my fault," Jessica protested.

"Too late to argue about that. Too late to argue about anything. Don't let it worry you. It doesn't matter. Nothing that happened 'down below' matters anymore. Please come in. Call me Pete. I'm happy to see you. We've been expecting you for quite a while."

"Sweet!" Matt exclaimed. "We get to go . . . in there!"

"Certainly! Come with me. I'll show you around. You're going to love it."

Jess and Matt followed Pete through the pearly gate. The people inside waved to them. Some had huge white wings attached to their shoulders. Most wore halos and long white robes, although a few had on different costumes. Very different costumes.

"Hey! That looks like Elvis!" Matt exclaimed.

"It *is* Elvis. Doesn't he look great? He's thin again." Pete waved to The King. "Yo, man! Looking good!"

"Thanks, man! Hey, anybody seen my band? We gotta start rehearsing. We got a gig coming up."

"No, man. But I'll let them know you're looking for them."

"Thanks, Pete. Stay righteous, brother!"

"See you later, alligator!"

Jessica swooned. "Wow! Grandma and Grandpa are never going to believe this. I saw Elvis!"

"How come some people wear robes and others don't? And why doesn't everybody have wings?" Matt asked.

"There's no dress code, if that's what you mean," Pete explained. "Some enjoy wearing a robe. Others prefer their own clothes. As for the wings, they're a badge of special achievement. They take a while to earn."

"What do you have to do?" Jessica asked.

"Follow me. I'll show you how to get started."

Pete led Matt and Jessica to a large white building. It looked like a cross between a church and a bank. Rows of tall columns lined the front. Pete pushed open the heavy bronze doors. Jess and Matt looked inside. It was a library. People walked here and there, taking thick books off endless shelves. Others sat at computer terminals, studying the information on the screen.

"Wow! You have the Internet here," Matt said.

"Of course!" Pete laughed. "As well as every significant book, poem, magazine article, and manuscript ever written. It's all here. Your halo is your library card. You can check out whatever you like, whenever you like. We're like Denny's. Open all night."

"Wow!" Matt exclaimed.

Jess seemed skeptical. "What about TV?"

"We don't have TV," Pete told her. "That's for the Other Place."

"How about videos?"

"Only if they're worthwhile and culturally uplifting."

"Music?"

"You'll find our rap collection rather limited, if that's what you're looking for."

"So what do you do around here besides hang out in the library?" Jess asked.

Pete chuckled. "I know what you're thinking. We don't force you to read books all the time. You and Matt will have the opportunity to take advantage of many learning experiences. Are you interested in dinosaurs, Matt?"

"Yeah!"

"Here you'll have the chance to actually see them. Professor Darwin will be happy to take you to visit our Jurassic site. How does that sound?"

"Cool!" Matt exclaimed.

"What about you, Jess? What learning experiences might you enjoy?"

Jess took several steps backward. "Oh no! I know what's happening! I just caught on. You don't fool me."

"What's the matter?" Matt asked.

"Figure it out, Matt! Where else do they talk about 'learning experiences' and 'educational opportunities'? Don't you get it? Don't you realize what this place is? It's *school!* Pete's gonna make us go to school *forever!*"

"Is that true?" Matt asked.

"It isn't as bad as all that," said Pete.

"Oh no?" said Jess. "What about lunch? Recess? Vacations? You don't have any of that, do you?"

"We don't need them," Pete tried to explain.

But Jess wouldn't let him. "It's school, Matt. S-C-H-O-O-L!!! You'll be in school until you're an old man with a long white beard. Like him!"

"Your friend's wrong, Matt," Pete said. "It's nothing at all like the schools you know. There are no tests or report cards. Nobody is ever forced to learn anything. Give it a chance! Wouldn't you like to see those dinosaurs? How about sailing on a real Viking ship with real Vikings? Or having Hans Christian Andersen or Robert Louis Stevenson tell you stories? Doesn't that sound exciting?"

Matt began to waver. "I know we need to find King Arthur, but couldn't we stay a little longer? I'd sure like to see those dinosaurs, Jess."

"Forget it! The quest comes first." Jessica turned to Pete. "Which way to the exit?"

"Go around the corner of the library. It's just down the stairs. Follow the sign until you come to the elevator. You can't miss it. Just remember, the elevator goes only one way. Down."

"I'm sorry, Pete," said Matt. "I wish I could stay."

"So do I," Pete replied. "But don't worry. You'll be back before you know it. Next time you'll be able to stay as long as you like."

"Ugh!" Jess exclaimed.

"You don't have to worry, Jessica. I'm sure we won't be seeing *you* for quite a while. If ever. I'll have to ask you to give back your halos. At least for now."

"Suits me," said Jess, handing back her golden ring.

Matt returned his reluctantly.

"Let's go, Matt. We're out of here."

Jess grabbed Matt's arm. She had to pull him all the way to the elevator. Then he tried to hold on to the columns.

"I want to see the dinosaurs!"

"Forget the dinosaurs. We'll rent *Jurassic Park*."

"It's not the same. And I want to sail on the Viking ship!"

"Who are you kidding? You got seasick when we

went on that whale-watching field trip. Now you want to be Conan the Barbarian?"

Matt began to cry. "I like this place, Jess. I don't want to go."

"We have to go," Jess insisted.

"Why?"

"Because we have a quest to complete. Are you going to leave Dennis and Lance in the lurch? We still don't know what happened to them. And how about King Arthur and all the others? Something very creepy is going on in Camelot, and we need to figure out what it is. We're the only ones who can do it. So the sooner we get back to medieval times, the better. This dump may look exciting, but it's a dead end. Real dead! If we're going to be trapped in a loop for a while, it might as well be someplace where we can have fun while we're figuring out how to escape. A place where we can stay up late, watch R-rated movies, eat high-calorie, high-cholesterol junk food. And no one ever, ever, ever makes us do homework or clean our rooms. We'll have a blast!"

"Are you sure?" Matt asked. He looked doubtful.

Jessica grinned. "Trust me!"

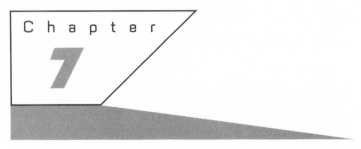

Chapter

7

# The Other Place

The digital numbers above the door flashed by in a glowing red blur as the elevator descended.

"How far down do we have to go?" Matt wondered.

Jess replied, "Considering where we're coming from, I'd expect a long trip."

"It's getting awfully warm," Matt said.

Jess answered, "I noticed."

*Screep!* The elevator jerked to a sudden halt. A computer voice announced, "Level Zero. Shopping Plaza. The GO-4 Mall Shopping Plaza features many exciting stores offering the latest in gift ideas for holiday giving. . . ." Matt and Jess stepped outside. The voice was still talking as the elevator doors shut.

"This isn't what I expected. Exactly where are we?" Matt asked.

"Whoa! Looks like a mall to me," Jess answered. "This is going to be better than I thought. Power shopping—yes! Let's go!"

Jess and Matt joined the crowds circling the plastic gardens in front of the shops. All their favorite stores were there—or almost there. Jess noticed that the names were not quite right: The Goop, New Army, Eddy Flower, Nerdstorm. People shuffled from store to store as if in a trance, dragging overflowing shopping bags, while Christmas music poured out over loudspeakers hidden in artificial palm trees.

"It sure doesn't seem like Christmas," Matt re-marked. There were no Santas, no friendly elves, no petting zoo. Nobody was smiling. Security guards in red suits with fake horns and tails hurried the crowds along with plastic pitchforks. "Only twenty more shopping days left . . . Move it along . . . Only twenty more—"

"Only twenty more days till what?" Matthew asked one of the guards.

"Who cares?" He shrugged. "Don't waste time talking. Do what you're supposed to do. Get out there and buy more stuff. Buy it all before it's gone. Buy, buy, buy!"

"Buy what?" Jessica asked the guard. She pointed to the bleak window displays. "Eight-track tape players? Disco formal wear? Pokey-Man videos? I can get better stuff at a garage sale!"

The guard lifted his walkie-talkie. "Code 7—Alert! Immediate assistance required. Station Twelve—Shopping Plaza. Refusal to buy." Red-suited security personnel began converging on the area. Shoppers milled around in confusion.

"What's going on?"

"Some kid refused to spend money!"

"That's *un-American!*"

"Uh-oh! Time to split." Jess grabbed Matt's

hand. Together they raced across the Shopping Plaza.

"Which way to the Cineplex?" Jess asked a smiling elf standing by the escalator. The elf pointed toward the second level. "Many exciting features are currently playing at our—" he began.

"Never mind," said Jess as she and Matt tore up the escalator.

"I thought all the elves were out of work," Matt said as they raced to the movie theater.

"That wasn't an elf. It was a cyber-elf. Can't you tell? Nobody real is that friendly. What's playing?" Jess asked the girl in the ticket booth.

The ticket seller looked like a life-size Barbie doll. She wiggled around in her seat and began speaking in a little girl voice: "Many wonderful features are currently playing at our new Cineplex theaters. In Theater A, we are showing *Gopher,* the exciting hit movie based on the lively computer game sweeping the nation. . . ."

"It isn't a hit, it isn't lively, and it isn't sweeping the nation," Jessica remarked.

The girl kept on talking, as if she hadn't heard a

word. "In Theater B we are showing *Gopher II,* the sequel to the exciting hit movie based on the lively computer game sweeping the nation. . . ."

"Is she for real?" Matt asked.

"Anatomically correct, yes," Jess answered. "Real? Definitely not!"

The ticket girl went right on babbling. *"Son of Gopher . . . Return of Gopher . . . Revenge of Gopher . . . Secret of Gopher . . . Mystery of Gopher . . . Beach Blanket Gopher . . ."*

"Forget it!" snapped Jess.

"What are we going to do now?" Matt asked. "We can't hide out in a movie theater if we can't stand the movies. Do you suppose the security guards are still looking for us?"

Jess peeked over the balcony. "Everybody's back in the stores. I think we're okay."

"Then let's get something to eat. I'm hungry," said Matt.


They walked around the corner to the Food Court. Matt stopped in front of the first counter. The sign above read: GOPHERBURGERS. Matt studied the menu hanging behind the cash register. "I'd like a hamburger," he said to the plastic clown behind the counter.

"What's the matter with you, kid? Can't you read?" snapped a voice from a speaker inside the clown's head. "No hamburgers. No cheeseburgers. Only Gopherburgers. Get it?"

"What's a Gopherburger?"

"If you knew, you wouldn't want one. Hurry up. I don't have all day."

"You don't have to be rude," Jessica said. "You'd better change your attitude, buster, or I'll ask to speak to the manager."

"I *am* the manager!" the clown snapped. "If you don't like it, lump it! You want friendly? Go see the purple dinosaur!"

"Let's go, Matt," said Jessica. "I wouldn't eat here if the food was free."

"But I'm hungry!" Matt whined. He turned to the clown. "Okay, I know what I want. Give me one Gopherburger with pickles and mustard. I'll have an order of Gopherfries with a Gophershake, too."

"You wanna supersize that?" the clown asked.

"Sure."

The clown burped. His stomach opened. Matt's order came sliding down the chute in a puddle of grease. The burger was the size of a dime, with no sign of pickles. The fries looked like sick worms. The shake was warm.

"This is supersize?" said Jess. "Then a microscope must come with a regular order—so you can see it!"

"That will be thirty-seven dollars and sixty-two cents," the clown said.

"For a burger, fries, and one tiny shake?" Matt was outraged. "That's ridiculous! We don't have that much money."

"Do you have a credit card?"

"No!"

"Want one?" The clown's chute opened. Two credit cards slid out.

"But we're kids. How can you give us credit cards?" Jess asked.

"Who says you need money to have a credit card?" the clown asked. "We give 'em away to

everybody: kids, homeless people, dogs, cats. Everybody gets a credit card."

"But what happens at the end of the month if people can't pay?"

"They get another credit card. It's called the global economy. Didn't anybody teach you that in school? Nobody ever has to pay for anything as long as they can get more credit. Don't try to figure it out. Just enjoy it . . . while it lasts."

"Awesome! We have credit cards!" Matt exclaimed, signing his name on the voucher.

"But there's nothing to buy," Jess protested.

"We'll find something. Let's eat first."

"I don't think so," said Jess. "Look what's coming up the escalator."

Two security guards in horns, tails, and red suits got off at the top. They began walking toward the Food Court.

"They must be on their lunch break. Time to disappear," said Matt.

"Where can we go?" Jess asked. Matt looked around.

"Over there! Tarbuck's Internet Café!"

.     .     .

Jess and Matt sneaked around the Food Court into the Internet Café. Rows of computers lined the tables along the walls. An espresso machine hissed in the corner. Signs on the wall proclaimed the wonders of Gopher-Mocha and Gopher-Latte.

"It smells like they brew it from compost," Jessica whispered to Matt. She walked up to the counter. A young man with greasy black hair and thick eyeglasses held together with duct tape sat before a monitor playing a computer game. He looked as if he hadn't slept in days. His thumbs slid back and forth across the gamepad. Jessica listened to the squeals coming from the speakers. She knew at once what game he was playing. Gopher.

Jessica and Matt waited several minutes. The young man, lost in the game, never looked up. Jess glanced out the café window. She saw a security guard talking to the plastic clown. She nudged Matt. "Here comes trouble. They're onto us. We better get out of here."

"Where can we go?" Matt whispered back.

"Don't worry. I have a plan." Jess rapped on the

monitor. "Hello! Hello in there! Anybody home?"

The young man looked up. "Oh, wow! People. I didn't see you come in. What do you want?"

"What do you have?"

He grinned. "We have neat-o video games."

"Like what?"

"Like Gopher. It's a terrific game. Have you ever played it?"

"Too many times. Keep going. What else?"

The young man blinked in surprise. "We don't have any other games. Why would you want other games when you can play Gopher?"

"The lights are on, but nobody's home," Jess murmured to Matt. "How about the Internet? This is Tarbuck's Internet Café, right?"

"Right! I can connect you, but it's expensive. It will cost you forty-five dollars a minute."

"Rip-off!" Matt exclaimed.

"Not to worry," said Jess. She threw her credit card on the counter. "Run it till it melts."

Jess took a seat at one of the computers and hit the <Shift> key. The monitor screen came to life.

Within seconds, she was on-line. She began typing.

"What are you doing?" Matt asked.

"Getting us out of here. I hate this place."

"I thought that might happen," said Matt. "Better hurry. Look who's coming!" Two security guards stormed through the door, carrying handcuffs and stun guns. Matt ducked so they wouldn't see him. Jess continued typing.

"Let's hope this is a fast connection," she said. "There! I've got it. **<Allgamescentral.org>**. Okay, now to find *Virtual Quest*. Scroll down to the *V*'s. *Vampire . . . Va-Va-Voom . . . Victory in the Desert* . . . Here it is."

"Hurry, Jess!" Matt pleaded.

"Don't rush me!" Jess snapped. "Okay! Here's what I want—a code that lets us jump levels. Enter sequence . . . players . . . got it." Matt glanced over his shoulder. He saw the young man pointing them out to the security guards.

"Faster, Jess! They're coming this way."

"Don't panic, Matt. What level do we want to go to?"

"I don't know!"

"How about Level Twelve? Does that sound good to you?"

"Anything sounds good to me!" Matt groaned as the security guards came striding across the room. One with yellow sergeant's stripes on his red sleeve held the cuffs. Matt heard him click on the stun gun.

"Okay, kids. You can come hard, or you can come easy; but either way, we're bringing you in," the sergeant said.

"What did we do, Officer?" Jessica chirped.

"Don't get smart with me, punk. Let's go."

"I don't think so," said Jess, typing in the numerals **<12>**.

"I said, let's go!" The guard pulled Jess out of her chair before she could enter the command. "Matt!" she yelled.

Matt lunged forward. The second guard grabbed his shirt collar. Matt felt the fabric tear as he hit the **<Enter>** key.

First the screen, then the whole room, went blank.

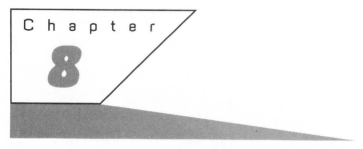

Chapter 8

# Trolls and Giants

Glowing red dots emerged from the darkness. As Matt and Jess watched, the dots formed themselves into loops and lines that gradually became letters. The letters read:

**Welcome to Level XII**
**The Dungeon**

"Terrific!" Matt cried. "Now you've done it! Look where you've gotten us this time. Why did you have to pick Level Twelve?"

"Oh, yeah? I don't recall hearing any better suggestions from you," Jess snapped. "Besides, nothing is ever so bad that it couldn't be worse. Level Thirteen might have been The Piranha Tank."

"It still could be," Matt grumbled.

The letters slowly dissolved. A scene began coming into view like a website appearing on a monitor screen. Unfortunately, it wasn't a pleasant scene. Doubly unfortunate, they were in it.

Level Twelve was indeed a dungeon. A deep, dark, dank, dismal, depressing dungeon. Its stone walls dripped with slime from leaky drains. The only light came from a tiny barred window in a heavy door studded with iron spikes. And it smelled! Jess and Matt held their noses. The straw heaped on the stone floor smelled worse than a soccer uniform that hadn't been washed in eight months.

"I think I'm going to throw up," Matt groaned.

"Go ahead," said Jessica. "It might improve the atmosphere. I wish we had yourgrocer.com. I'd order a year's supply of Odor-Eaters." Suddenly, she gasped. "What's that?"

The straw began to move.

Before Jess's and Matt's astonished eyes, a figure arose from the straw. It unfolded itself limb by limb—knees, hips, back, shoulders, neck—until it stood erect in the middle of the room. Or nearly erect. It had to stoop so that its head wouldn't bump the ceiling.

"A giant!" Matt and Jess screamed together.

"Quiet!" the giant snapped. "Don't make so much noise. You'll bring the guards, and we don't want that. No sir! Another dose of 'Reeducation' and I'll be walking around on my knuckles. Sorry to see you here, kids. We all hoped you'd gotten away."

"Who's 'we'?" Jess asked. The giant's voice sounded familiar, although she couldn't see his face, hidden as it was in the dark shadows of the vaulted ceiling.

"Me and Lance and Dennis. That's why there's all this straw. The guards brought it in for the horses. The trouble is they didn't take it out after the horses left. And they didn't change it even once the whole three months Dennis and Lance were here!"

"That's cruel and unusual punishment," said Matt. "Where are Dennis and Lance now?"

"Who knows?" the giant answered. "The guards took them out one day for questioning. They never came back."

"Oh no! I hope nothing awful happened to them."

"In a place like this, you know something awful happened to them. What you have to hope for is that nothing really, really, really, *really* awful happened to them."

Jessica interrupted. "Excuse me, Mr. Giant, or whatever your name is. I need to ask a question. Have we met before? You seem to know us, but I can't quite place you."

"Yeah," Matt added. "We've met centaurs and knights and elves since we started this quest. But no giants. I'm positive of that."

"Aw, you hurt my feelings, kids. Don't you know who I am? We met in the forest. Of course, I wasn't a giant then. I was an elf. Elfric the Elf. Remember me now? I asked you for a handout."

"You're the elf?" Matt gasped.

"That's right. You gave me a banana."

At first, Jess was too surprised to speak. "How'd you get to be so huge? You were only three feet tall when we met you!"

"The troll gang that runs this dungeon gave me 'The Treatment,' " Elfric explained. "They put me on the rack and stretched me, to pay me back for all the times I kicked them out of Elf Acres. That's why it looks like I'm wearing shorts and a T-shirt—these were my regular clothes when they started. They only stopped stretching me when I got too tall to fit on the rack. I had the last laugh, though. They could stretch me, but they couldn't break me. I didn't tell them anything."

"What did they want to find out?" Matt asked.

"Where you were. I couldn't tell them anything because I didn't know anything. Uh-oh! I better shut up. Somebody's coming."

Heavy keys rattled in the lock. Rusty hinges squealed as the door swung open. In walked a troll.

He was only as tall as a trash can, but every inch bulged with muscles. His nose hung down to his waist, and it was pierced with an astounding collection of spikes, studs, and rings. His ears carried their own arsenal of heavy metal. Two snake tattoos circled up each arm and around his biceps. An iron ring loaded with keys hung from a hook on his belt. He carried a picnic basket covered with a blue gingham napkin.

"Here's lunch," the troll growled. "Enjoy it while you can." He handed Matt the picnic basket.

"What's on the menu?" Jess asked.

"Same thing that's on the menu every day. Gopherburgers, Gopherfries, and one lukewarm Gophershake. Haw, Haw, Haw!"

"You just killed my appetite," said Matt.

"Too bad!" the troll replied. "You should try to eat something. You're a growing boy. And you're really gonna be growing in another half hour, as soon as we get the Stretcher set up. Catch you later, Stretch! Haw, haw, haw!"

The troll shuffled out into the passageway. Matt

and Jess heard the keys jangle as he locked the door.

"What now?" Matt asked Jess.

"Don't know," she answered. "I think we're in serious trouble. There's no way out. Did anyone ever escape from this place?" she asked Elfric.

"Nobody that I know," the elf replied.

Matt sighed. "I hate these stinky Gopher-burgers."

"Don't talk to me about stinky," the elf replied. "Gopherburgers give me terrible gas. Sometimes I feel as if I ate one of these." He reached into his pocket and took out a blaster bomb.

"Ohmigosh!" Jess yelped. "You still have the one I gave you?"

"The trolls captured me before I could turn it in. I figured I'd better hold on to it, just in case."

"I didn't think blaster bombs worked in the Middle Ages," Matt remarked.

"Oh, they work!" the elf replied. "We're just not supposed to have them."

"Why didn't you blast open the dungeon door and escape?" Jess asked.

"To where?" Elfric replied. "The trolls come running, and what am I supposed to do? I'm only an elf. You saw the muscles on that guy. I'm weak, strung out on Gopherburgers. I can't fight them all."

"Didn't they search you when they brought you in?"

"No. Trolls are kind of stupid. They take a lot of those steroids, you know, to build up their muscles. I think it makes them dumber. And meaner."

"This is perfect!" Matt said. "Listen up, guys. I think I know how to get us out of this dungeon. Don't ask me to explain. Just do what I say. Give me the bomb. When the troll comes back, I want him to find us all dancing around, as if we were listening to music."

"What kind of music?" asked Jess.

"Jazz, rock—it doesn't matter. Just dance."

"What about ELMFRE?" Elfric asked.

"What's ELMFRE?"

"Easy Listening Music for Romantic Elves. We have a lot of nice tunes. You may know some of them. 'Little Things Mean a Lot'? 'There's a Small Hotel'? 'Tiny Bubbles'?"

"Dance to whatever you like," said Matt. "When that troll comes through the door, pretend you're listening and moving to music. Leave the rest to me."

Matt had hardly finished speaking when they heard the keys rattling again. "Get set. Here he comes!" he whispered. Jess and Elfric began dancing around in circles, snapping their fingers. Matt held the blaster bomb to his ear and pranced around, too.

"I love you. You love me . . ."

"Oooh! Oooh! Don't want no scrubs . . . can't get no love . . ." chirped Jess.

Elfric hunched his shoulders and swiveled his hips, crooning, "Little Sister, don't you . . . Little Sister, don't you . . ." He was surprisingly graceful for someone who was twelve feet tall.

The troll's jaw dropped. "Well, who tied the pup? What in blue blazes is going on here?"

"We're dancing," Matt told him.

"To what? I don't hear any music," the troll replied.

"To this!" Matt showed him the blaster bomb. "Haven't you ever seen one of these before? It's what we call an MP3 player. You load it with whatever music you like, and it plays it back for you."

"Where do you get the music from?"

"Off the Internet. Through the phone lines. The Web's full of music. But you need one of these to hear it."

Matt might have been speaking Tadjik or Croatian for all the troll understood. Nonetheless, Matt succeeded in getting him interested. "Can I listen?" he asked.

"Sure," said Matt, handing him the blaster bomb. "See this little pin. You twist it to change the program. If you want to make it real loud, pull it all the way."

The troll held the bomb to his ear. "I don't hear anything."

"Just listen," Matt told him. "You have to give it

a second for your ears to adjust. All the metal in your ears and nose may be causing static."

"I still don't hear anything." The troll was trying so hard to listen that he failed to notice Jess and Elfric slipping behind him.

"Scooby-dooby-doo," Jess began.

Elfric came in with the harmony. "A-rama-lama-ding-dong!"

"Hey! This is cool! I can hear it now," the troll said. "Okay, that's enough. All three of you, stop dancing. I'm confiscating this MPP or whatever you call it."

"You can't do that!" Matt whined.

"Sure I can! I'm taking it down to the guard-room for closer examination. I'll be back in a few minutes. I'd suggest you do some *stretching* exercises in the meantime. Haw, haw, haw!"

The troll slammed the door behind him as he hurried down the passageway. "Hey, kid!" he called back to Matt. "How do I make it louder?" His voice echoed off the stone walls.

"Pull the pin and hold it to your ear!" Matt called through the bars.

"I still can't hear anything."

"Pull the pin harder."

"Hey! It fell out!"

"That's okay! Hold it to your ear. You'll hear music soon."

"Yeah! Real soon," said Jess. She crouched in the straw with Matt and Elfric.

"All together now," said Matt. "A-bee-bop-a-looba! A-bop-bam—"

# BOOM!

The explosion rattled the dungeon walls. The door blew open. Bits of rock and mortar rained down from the ceiling.

"Okay, guys! We're out of here!" Matt yelled to Jess and Elfric. The giant bumped his head on the lintel as he raced out the door. "Ow!" he yelped. "I keep forgetting to duck."

"Remember—from now on, think *big!*" Matt suggested.

"Which way?" Jess asked. The passage to the left dripped with bits of smashed troll. The one to the right ended in another heavy door studded with iron spikes. Stuck on one of the spikes was a parchment sign reading:

DANGER

ENTRANCE FORBIDDEN

AUTHORIZED PERSONNEL ONLY

TRESPASSERS WILL BE DRAWN AND

QUARTERED

"That way!" said Matt.

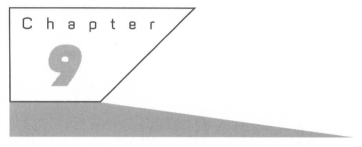

Chapter

9

# Chamber of Secrets

The door was locked. "What now?" Jess asked.

"The troll had that big ring of keys hanging from his belt. Maybe one of them opens this door," Matt suggested.

"Do you want to go hunt for it?" They looked at each other.

"Eeeeuuuuuw!"

"Step aside, kids," said Elfric. He grasped the door handle in his giant fist. He gave one mighty tug that ripped the handle and the whole locking mechanism out of the door. But it still wouldn't open.

"There must be a magic spell holding it shut," Matt said.

"What do we do?" Jess and Elfic asked him.

"You fight fire with fire," Matt began, "and magic with magic!" He reached in his pocket and pulled out a magic wand. It glowed and sparkled in the corridor's dim light.

Jess gasped. "Where did you get that?"

"It's the one Dennis gave me. I picked it up when the Merrie Men started fighting."

"You mean you had it all along? Why didn't you tell us? We could have turned the trolls into toads and walked right out of that dungeon."

Matt shrugged. "I didn't think we needed it. Video games are lots more fun when you use your brains instead of piles of special junk. I was saving the magic wand for when we got really stuck."

"Well, we're really stuck now," said Jess. "So make with some hocus-pocus to get this game rolling."

"Yeah! Let's move it, guys! Think big!" added Elfric.

"Think big!" Matt echoed. He rapped on the door with his magic wand . . . and it disappeared.

"Onward and upward!" yelled Jess, entering the empty doorway. "Think big! But don't forget to duck your head."

The questers and their giant companion inched their way up a winding staircase. They had to feel their way in the darkness. Spiderwebs brushed against their faces, and unseen skittering things crunched underfoot.

"Eeeeeuuuuuuw!" Jess squealed when an extra large one went *squish!*

"I'm glad they don't jump," said Matt.

"Keep going! I see light. We must be getting to the end," Elfric called out.

The stairs led to another locked door. "I'll use my magic wand," said Matt.

"No way!" said Elfric. "Let's save the magic for emergencies. This one's mine! Stand back!" He smashed the door to splinters with one kick. "Think big!"

"Cool!" Matt exclaimed.

Jess poked her head through the shattered doorway. "Whoa! Look at this!"

They entered a hallway like nothing they had encountered so far. It belonged more to a modern office building than a medieval castle. There was a rest room, a watercooler, fluorescent lights, blue carpeting on the floor, and motivational posters hanging on the blue pastel walls.

*THE DARK AGES ARE OVER*

*WE'RE NOT MEDIEVAL ANYMORE*

*UNARMOR YOUR MIND*

*COMMITMENT IS THE SOURCE OF SOURCERY*

"They spelled *sorcery* wrong," Matt said.

"Maybe spelling was looser in the Middle Ages," Jess suggested.

"What's spelling?" asked Elfric.

"That answers your question," said Matt.

They stopped before an elevator. "I wonder where this goes?" Jess pushed the UP button. The door opened. Jess, Matt, and Elfric walked in. The door closed behind them.

"Now what?" Elfric asked. He had never been in an elevator.

"Now we pick our floor," said Jess. "Let's go to the top." She pressed the button for 13.

The elevator began rising. "Help! Sorcery! Witchcraft!" Elfric yelled.

"No. Elevator," Jess said. "We ride these all the time. It's an easy way of getting from one floor to another, if you don't want to take the stairs."

"Especially when the stairs are covered with squishy bugs," Matt added.

The elevator stopped on the thirteenth floor. The doors opened. Matt and Jess poked their heads out and peered down the hallway. This one was bare. No posters, no watercooler, no signs, no rest room. Only the same blue pastel walls and blue carpet leading down the hall to another door. Written across the panels of highly polished wood in bright gold letters were the words:

*EXECUTIVE SUITE*

"I'll handle this. Stand back!" said Elfric. He gave the door a mighty kick. Nothing happened.

"I'll make it disappear," said Matt. He touched the door with his magic wand. The wand sparked and glowed, but the door remained where it was.

"Chill, guys!" said Jess. "Something tells me this isn't an ordinary door. Trying to force our way in won't work."

"What if we knock?" Matt suggested.

"Go ahead."

Matt knocked. No answer.

"Is there a telephone or speaker somewhere? Maybe we have to call the receptionist first."

They looked all around for a telephone, speaker, buzzer. Nothing.

"What's this?" Elfric had discovered a small door, only a few inches square. They hadn't noticed it at first because it was painted the same blue pastel color as the walls. Jess opened it. Inside she saw three rows of numbered buttons.

$$1 \quad 2 \quad 3$$
$$4 \quad 5 \quad 6$$
$$7 \quad 8 \quad 9$$

"I don't get it," the giant said.

"It's an electronic lock," Matt explained. "You punch in the code, and the door opens."

"But what's the code?" asked Jess. "Those nine numbers have millions of possible combinations. We could stand here forever and still not get the right one."

"Then we're stuck," Elfric sighed.

"No, wait," said Matt. "This reminds me of something I read on a website about computer security. The topic was passwords. Most people use simple, obvious passwords so they can remember them easily. They shouldn't, but they do. So if someone were to go through the bother of installing an electronic lock in a place where toilet paper is an important technological breakthrough, they might not bother with an elaborate code. What's the point, when hardly anyone can read or write? A simple word would do."

"Like what?" Jess asked.

"Like **Open**," said Matt.

"But there aren't any letters. Only numbers."

"There are letters on a telephone. Help me out.

Can you remember what letters go with which buttons?"

Jess closed her eyes. "Wait! I think I have it. There's nothing under 1. The alphabet begins with 2. It's three letters for each button till you get to 9."

"Okay, let's figure it out," said Matt. "O would be 6. P would be 7."

"E would be 3 . . ." said Jess.

"And N would take you back to 6," said Elfric.

"How'd you know that?" Jess and Matt asked.

"I may be medieval, but my brain isn't in the Dark Ages," Elfric said. "I've been to school."

"So the code is: 6-7-3-6," said Matt. He punched in the numbers.

A computer voice came from a hidden speaker overhead. "Please state your name and authorization number."

"Matthew the Great. 386-45731-89932."

"What number is that?" Jess asked.

"I made it up. If it doesn't work, we'll try something else. That's how hackers break into the Pentagon, except they have random-number generating programs to help them. We may not need a specific number at all. Whoever coded the lock may have left this option blank. It'll accept any number."

"My turn," said Jess. She gave her name and number. "Jessica the Lionhearted. 888-88-88888."

"Now me," said Elfric. "The Giant Formerly Known as Elfric the Elf. XVIIII-CDVIII-XIVDC-IIIVI."

"You may enter," the voice said. The door slid noiselessly into the wall.

"Some security system!" Jess exclaimed as she, Matt, and Elfric stepped into a darkened space. "I'm glad that the nerds who set it up don't work for our government. Or maybe they do!" The door slid back into place behind them.

"Where are we? It's awfully dark," Matt whispered. His voice disappeared in the emptiness.

"It's awfully big, too," said Jess. "I can't feel the walls."

"I can't feel the ceiling," said Elfric.

Blinding lights suddenly struck their eyes. A deep voice rumbled from powerful speakers.

*"Welcome to the Chamber of Secrets!"*

A gigantic figure floated in midair. Clad in a dark-blue robe and a pointed hat spangled with stars, it waved an ebony wand tipped with a metal ball. Red and blue laser beams shot from its eyes. A wind began to blow. The speakers howled with the roar of a hurricane. Mighty gusts whipped the figure's long, white beard like a flapping sail.

*"Do you know who I am?"*

"Holy moley!" said Matt. "It's Merlin!"

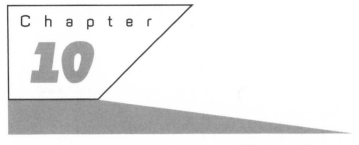

# Showdown

"Wrong!" The figure's voice became a croaking rattle. "I'm Marlon, Merlin's evil clone! I'm a greater wizard than Merlin ever was, or could ever hope to be!"

"So you're the one who's been messing up Camelot and letting Merlin take the rap. That shows a lot of character. I'm real impressed," said Jess.

"If you're Marlon, where's Merlin?" cried Matt.

"There he is, with all your other friends!"

A glowing disk appeared in midair, shining like the surface of a mirror. Matt and Jess saw faces spinning within its depths.

"It's King Arthur and Queen Guinevere! And Merlin the Magician. The *real* Merlin!" Elfric exclaimed.

Matt and Jess had no trouble recognizing the other two.

"Dennis! Lance! What are you doing in there?"

" 'Tis a long story that would taketh too much time to telleth," said Lance.

"We're all in a jam, little buddies: King Arthur, Queen Guinevere, Merl, Lance, and me," Dennis pleaded. "You're the only ones who can get us out. It's up to you, buds. If you blow it, the evil clone dude wins."

"Today, Camelot! Tomorrow the world—past, present, and future!" Marlon bellowed.

"How'd you all get into this mess?" Matt asked.

"The fault is mine," groaned Merlin. "Not long ago, I set out upon a quest into the future. I wished to learn what lay ahead for the human race. After many adventures in the Land of Cal-Ee-Forn-Ya, I came to an enchanted realm called the Valley of Silicon. There I met other wizards who invited me to join them in creating marvels. I helped them to create a game; a wonderful, enchanting game for families to play together. The challenge was to eliminate a host of terrible little animals who live in burrows beneath the greensward."

"Gopher!" Jess gasped.

The wizard continued. "One day I made a terrible mistake. In a moment of foolishness, for lack of anything better to do, I pressed my face against a magical device called a scanner. My image went into an enchanted box called a computer hard drive and appeared on a magic screen called a monitor. I discovered that by using the computer's tools I could make myself short or tall, fat or thin. Little did I know there was an evil spirit called a virus lurking in the hard drive. It took my image without my knowledge and transformed it into another being: Marlon, an evil wizard who possessed all my knowledge but none of my strength of character. When I returned to Camelot, Marlon, like a hidden flea on a dog, came with me. Assuming my appearance, he began advising King Arthur and Queen Guinevere. He gave orders in my name. Before any of us realized who he was, we were all his prisoners. Now here we are, trapped within Marlon's Silver Circle, helpless to stop his plan to invade the twenty-first century."

"Marlon's coming to our time?" Matt gasped.

"Of course!" Marlon echoed. "Why would I stay in the Middle Ages? There's no cable, no cell phones, no fast food, no VCRs. It's a dump! They don't have washing machines or showers. They don't even have toilets!"

"What about computer games?" Jess asked. "I'll bet you miss them."

"Do I! I love computer games. I invented computer games. Did you ever hear of a game called Gopher? That's my game. I invented it. It's the greatest, most exciting game in history!"

"Beg to differ," said Jess. "Merlin says he and his friends in Silicon Valley invented it. Anyhow, that's not something I'd brag about. It's not like you thought up Quake or Doom. Gopher's a bust. A bore, a game for babies. Me and my friends laugh at Gopher. Dweebs play Gopher. Gopher is a game for losers!"

"Is not!"

"Is too!" Matt agreed.

Jess continued. "It's down to this, Marlon. I remember a show I saw once on the History Channel. When people in the Middle Ages had a problem they couldn't settle any other way, they challenged each other to Trial by Combat. They or their champions would fight to the finish. The winner was judged to be in the right. So, Mr. Wizard, I challenge you to Trial by Gopher. I bet I can beat your pants off, or your boxer shorts, or whatever you wear under that dorky bathrobe. If I win, you have to free Merlin, King Arthur, Queen Guinevere, Lance, and Dennis. You have to turn Lance back into a knight and restore Elfric to his proper size."

"Wait a minute," said Elfric. "I'm getting used to being a giant. I love thinking big! I'm not sure I want to be a shrimp again."

"Elfric can decide whatever he wants," Jess went on. "As for you, Marlon, you agree to return to cyberspace and not hassle anyone in Camelot ever again."

"And if I beat you?" Marlon thundered.

"Then everyone remains where they are and what

they are, and you can do whatever you like to my best bud, Matt."

"Wait just a minute!" Matt shouted. But before he could say another word, Marlon answered, "Agreed!"

"Are you sure you know what you're doing? It's my neck you're playing with," Matt hissed at Jess.

"Forsooth, thou art one brave girl," King Arthur said.

"Most noble, too," Queen Guinevere agreed.

"Of matchless beauty," Lancelot added.

"And rare intelligence," said Merlin.

"Don't let this sweet talk go to your head, babe," said Dennis. "We're not out of here yet. We may all end up busted."

"Maybe you should borrow my magic wand," Matt whispered. "Just in case."

"No way," said Jess. "Trust me, guys. I know what I'm doing. I can beat that cyber-sucker blindfolded with both hands tied behind my back."

A fanfare of trumpets blared. Marlon announced, "Let the game begin!"

An overhead spotlight clicked on. The floor

opened. A computer console with a keyboard and gamepad rose into a circle of intense light. A giant monitor descended from the ceiling. A thick red line split the screen. The bar over the right side read **<Marlon, World's Greatest Wizard>**.

"Type in your name," Marlon commanded.

Jessica's fingers tapped and tapped at the keyboard.

"What's taking so long?" Marlon grumbled.

"Don't rush me," said Jess, clicking away. "It's hard finding the letters in the dark." At last, the words **<Jessica, Wizard Stomper>** appeared in the bar over her side. She hit **<Return>**. The screen went black. The Gopher movie began. Thousands of mutant gophers assembled in their underground tunnels. Their leader, Saddam Adolf Fidel Gopher, gave his speech about conquering the world for Gopherdom. Then the gophers swarmed up the tunnels to do battle with unsuspecting suburbanites.

"This movie gets more lame every time I see it," Jess commented.

"Are you sure you don't want to borrow my magic wand?" Matt asked. "Marlon's going to be awfully tough to beat. He knows all the tricks, and he probably plays dirty, too. Take the wand, Jess. You're going to need it."

"Nope," Jess told Matt. "I'm going to beat that sucker with brains and courage. That's the real challenge of playing video games. You said that back in the dungeon, and you're right. Who needs all the other junk? Uh-oh! Out of the way, Matt. Here they come!"

Jess's thumbs flew over the gamepad. On the screen, her riding mower whizzed across the lawn, turning gophers into sushi as they poured from their tunnels. The score bar at the top of the screen whirled off the numbers. Then the gophers started shooting back. Jessica found herself dodging rockets and artillery shells.

"Heat shield time," cried Jess as she clicked on the protection panels. "Give me some blasters!" She started shooting back, tossing grenades and blaster bombs left and right. "How am I doing, Matt!" she yelled.

"Keep going! You're beating Marlon by eleven

thousand points. Duck, Jess! They have missiles."

The gophers poured fire at Jessica. Jessica fired back as her lawn mower skidded across the lawn in wild zigzags, mashing and blasting the gophers. For every one she squashed, hundreds more poured from the tunnels. Jess glanced at Marlon's screen. He was ahead by 22,000 points. His lawn mower zipped over the lawn. The gophers couldn't touch him, even though he hadn't even turned on his heat shields. Jess couldn't help admiring his technique. The wizard clone was a terrific gamer.

"Time to end this," she muttered, turning her lawn mower around and racing for the gas pump. The gophers pursued her, firing as they came.

"Jess! What are you doing?" Matt squealed as Jess stuck the nozzle in the nearest tunnel and pumped gasoline down the hole. "Your shields are almost gone! You can't fire back when you're at the pump! You're gonna get creamed! Take the wand! Please take it!"

"No way!"

Matt covered his eyes. He couldn't bear to watch

what would surely happen when Jessica's shields came down and the gophers, blackening the screen, hit her with everything they had.

"Anybody got a match?" said Jess. Her screen went up in a blaze of red. When the smoke cleared, the lawn was gone. So were the gophers. She had racked up 275,864,801,649,241 points. Marlon's score didn't even come close.

"I win!" said Jess, taking a bow.

"That was incredible!" Matt exclaimed. "How did you do it? You used up your shields. You couldn't fire back. You had no special magic. The gophers blasted you with everything they had, but they kept missing!"

"Easy!" said Jess. "<45-128-makemeimmortal>. It works every time!"

"That's the cheat code! No fair!" Marlon roared.

"Oh yes, it is," said King Arthur. "I, as ruler of Camelot, am also Herald King of Arms. I decide all questions of chivalry. There are no rules in Trial by Combat. All is fair. The winner is the one left standing. Since Jessica wiped out the gophers and accumulated MMMCCCCDDDDLXXXXVIII more points than the false and faithless wizard Marlon, I declare her to be the winner."

"Horse patooties!" Marlon snapped. "You're all a bunch of fossils. What do I care what you think? You're my prisoners anyway, so the only decision around here that counts is mine. And I say that all bets are off."

"Say whatever you like," said Jess, staring at the wizard face-to-face. "I know what you are, Marlon. You don't scare me. You're not really here. You're just a hologram projected in the middle of the room. You're not even a real person. You're only a file on your computer's hard drive. And I'm in your computer now, so I think I'll take a look around."

"No! You wouldn't dare!" Marlon shouted.

"Wouldn't I?" said Jess. She clicked **<Quit>** to exit the game. The desktop appeared. She clicked on an icon labeled Wizard Secrets. "I wonder what's in here?" she said.

"You'll never find out. You can't get in," Marlon sneered. "You need the password. And you won't get it from me."

"Maybe not," said Jess. "On the other hand, I have a hunch as to what it might be."

A dialog box appeared on the screen.

---

*Restricted Folder: Wizard Secrets*
*Enter password:*

---

"Let's try this and see if it works." Jess began entering the letters: **g-o-p** . . .

"Stop! What are you doing?" Marlon screamed.

"I'm entering your password, cloneface." Jessica continued typing: **h-e-r.**

The file opened.

"Stop! Get out!" Marlon demanded. "You have no right to be here. These are my private files. My personal records!"

Jess ignored him. "This one looks interesting. **<Merlin.clone.jpeg>.** Shall we open it, Matt?"

"Don't, Jess. We don't know what's in there."

"You're right. It could be a whole nest of viruses. We better not let any loose to cause more trouble. So maybe we better dump the whole file . . . in the trash!"

"No! No! N—" Marlon screamed. His voice stopped; his image vanished as Jessica dragged the *Wizard Secrets* file to the Trash.

"Let's make sure he doesn't come back," she said, clicking on **<Delete>**.

"Marlon's history!" Matt and Elfric shouted, jumping with joy.

"Don't forget about us, dudes!" Dennis cried. He, Lancelot, Merlin, King Arthur, and Queen Guinevere were still prisoners within the enchanted Silver Circle.

"I think I know how to break the spell," said Jess. She clicked on the Silver Circle icon on the desktop and dragged it to the Trash. Something inside the computer clicked. The CD-ROM tray slid open. "Here's your magic Silver Circle. It's no big deal." Jess took the CD-ROM disk from the tray and snapped it in two.

All the lights went out. The computer screen turned black. They came back on again within a moment, and when they did, Marlon's prisoners were standing in the middle of the room.

"The evil spell is broken! We're free!" they cried.

"Alas! I am still a horse!" groaned Lance.

"Oh, crabcakes! I don't know how to fix that," said Jess. "And Elfric is still a giant. Maybe we can check the chatrooms. Somebody might have an idea of what to do."

"I will give the matter my full attention," Merlin said. "I'm sure my magic books will lead me to the answer."

"Don't bother," said Elfric. "I like being bigger than everyone else. It's not so bad once you get used to it. Let's see what they say at the mall when I ask for a job now!"

"And you need to loosen up, dude!" Dennis told Lance. "Tell you what? Why don't we catch the Horse Show? We can hang out with the Thoroughbreds, flirt with the fillies. Life's for living, Lance. You can't spend your whole life in an iron suit."

"Perhaps thou are right, noble-hearted half-horse friend," Lance agreed. "Perhaps one ought to stoppeth from time to time to smelleth the clover."

"How can we ever repay you?" said Queen Guinevere to Jess and Matt.

"I will knight you both, and enter you into the

rolls of the Order of the Round Table," King Arthur said. "We will hold a tournament in your honor, the greatest ever held within Camelot's walls. We will feast for seven days and seven nights."

"Thanks, everybody. Matt and I had a great time here. We wish we could stay, but we really have to get home," said Jess.

"Yeah," Matt agreed. "I have homework, and Jess has soccer practice."

"Come back soon!" everyone told them. Matt and Jess waved good-bye.

"How do we get out of here?" Matt asked.

"Same way you get out of any game," said Jess. "Pull down the **<File>** menu and hit **<Quit>**."

"Okay," said Matt, moving the cursor across the screen.

"Matt! What did you just do?"

"You said hit **<Quit>**. I hit **<Quit>**."

"No you didn't! You hit **<New Game>**," Jess said as the room and screen suddenly went dark.

"Oh, no!" cried Matt as computer music began pouring from the speakers. "Here we go again!"